Angelina Ballerina

Illustrations by Helen Craig Text by Katharine Holabird

A TRUMPET CLUB SPECIAL EDITION

More than anything else in the world, Angelina loved to dance. She danced all the time and she danced everywhere, and often she was so busy dancing that she forgot about the other things she was supposed to be doing.

Angelina's mother was always calling her, "Angelina, it's time to straighten up your room now," or "Please get ready for school now, Angelina." But Angelina never wanted to go to school. She never wanted to do anything but dance.

One night Angelina even danced in her dreams, and when she woke up in the morning, she knew that she was going to be a real ballerina some day.

When Mrs. Mouseling called Angelina for breakfast,
Angelina was standing on her bed doing curtsies.

When it was time for school, Angelina was trying on her mother's hats and making sad and funny faces at herself in the mirror. "You're going to be late again, Angelina!" cried Mrs. Mouseling.

But Angelina did not care. She skipped over rocks

and practiced high leaps over the flowerbeds until she landed right in old

Mrs. Hodgepodge's pansies and got a terrible scolding.

At playtime she twirled and spun across the playground so fast that none of the little boys in her class could catch up with her and they were all very cross.

After school she did a beautiful arabesque in the kitchen and knocked over a pitcher of milk and a plate of her mother's best Cheddar cheese pies.

"Oh Angelina, your dancing is nothing but a nuisance!"
exclaimed her mother.

She sent Angelina straight upstairs to her room and went to have a talk with Mr. Mouseling. Mrs. Mouseling shook her head and said, "I just don't know what to do about Angelina." Mr. Mouseling thought awhile and then he said, "I think I may have an idea."

That same afternoon Mr. and Mrs. Mouseling went out
together before the shops closed.

The next morning at breakfast Angelina found a large
box with her name on it.

Inside the box was a pink ballet dress and a pair of pink ballet slippers. Angelina's father smiled at her kindly. " I think you are ready to take ballet lessons, " he said.

Angelina was so excited that she jumped straight up in the air and landed with one foot in her mother's sewing basket.

The very next day Angelina took her pink slippers and ballet dress and went to her first lesson at Miss Lilly's Ballet School. There were nine other little girls in the class and they all practiced curtsies and pliés and ran around the room together just like fairies. Then they skipped and twirled about until it was time to go home.

"Congratulations, Angelina," said Miss Lilly. "You are a good little dancer and if you work hard you may grow up to be a real ballerina one day."

Angelina ran all the way home to give her mother a big
hug. "I'm the happiest little girl in the world today!"
she said.

From that day on, Angelina came downstairs when her mother called her, she straightened up her room, and she went to school on time.

She helped her mother
make Cheddar cheese pies

and she even let the boys catch her
in the playground sometimes.

Angelina was so busy dancing at Miss Lilly's that she
didn't need to dance at suppertime or bedtime or on the
way to school any more. She went every day to her
ballet lessons and worked very hard for many years

. . . until at last she became the famous ballerina, Mademoiselle Angelina, and people came from far and wide to enjoy her lovely dancing.

Published by
The Trumpet Club
666 Fifth Avenue
New York, New York 10103

Text copyright © 1983 by Katharine Holabird
Illustrations copyright © 1983 by Helen Craig

ISBN: 0-440-84488-6

Reprinted by arrangement with Clarkson N. Potter, Inc./Publishers
Printed in the United States of America
January 1989

10 9 8 7 6 5 4 3 2